Favorite Pets

Story by Jenna Winterberg • Illustrations by Diana Fisher

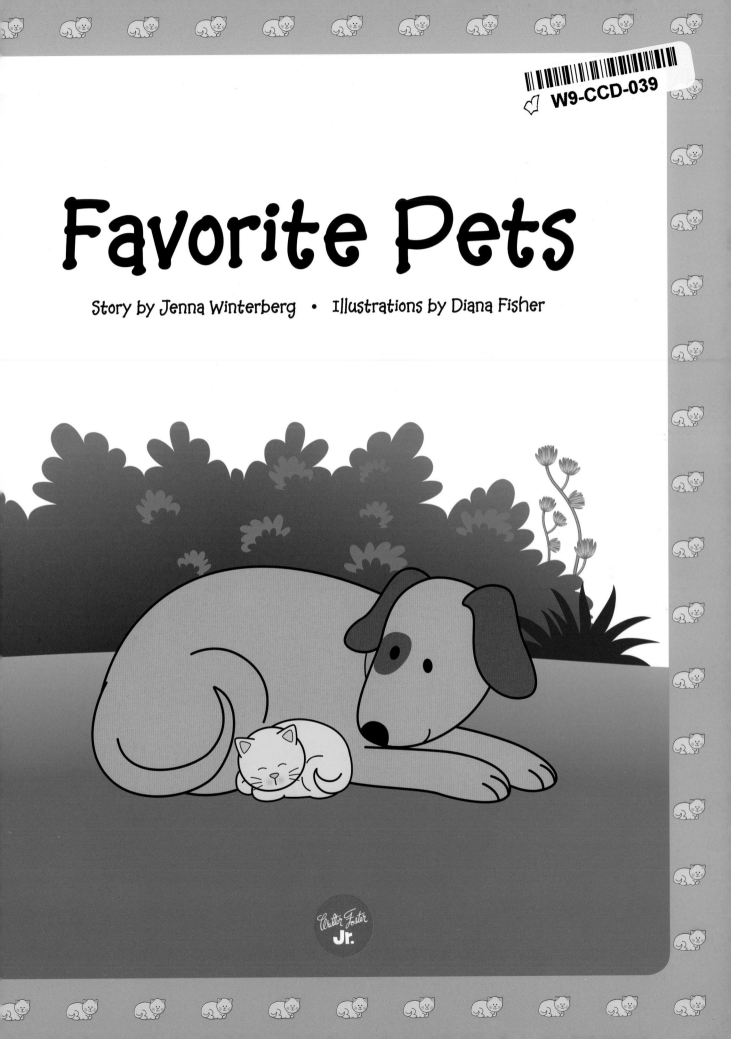

Walter Foster Jr.

Meet Boomer. Boomer lives with the Bailey family. The Baileys give him a lot of love and attention. They feed him, walk him, and pet him regularly. The Baileys also play games with Boomer, and Boomer watches over the whole Bailey household. It's a dog's life, and Boomer loves it!

Draw Boomer the dog!

When you finish your drawing, place the ball sticker on the opposite page!

Boomer's best friend is a kitten named Mew. Mew is very young, so she doesn't know the rules of the house yet. For example, she climbs on the kitchen counters and naps on Mr. Bailey's favorite chair! But because Mew is Boomer's best friend, he never tattles. When the Baileys find fur in all the wrong places, they blame Boomer. "BOO-MER!"

Draw Mew the Kitten!

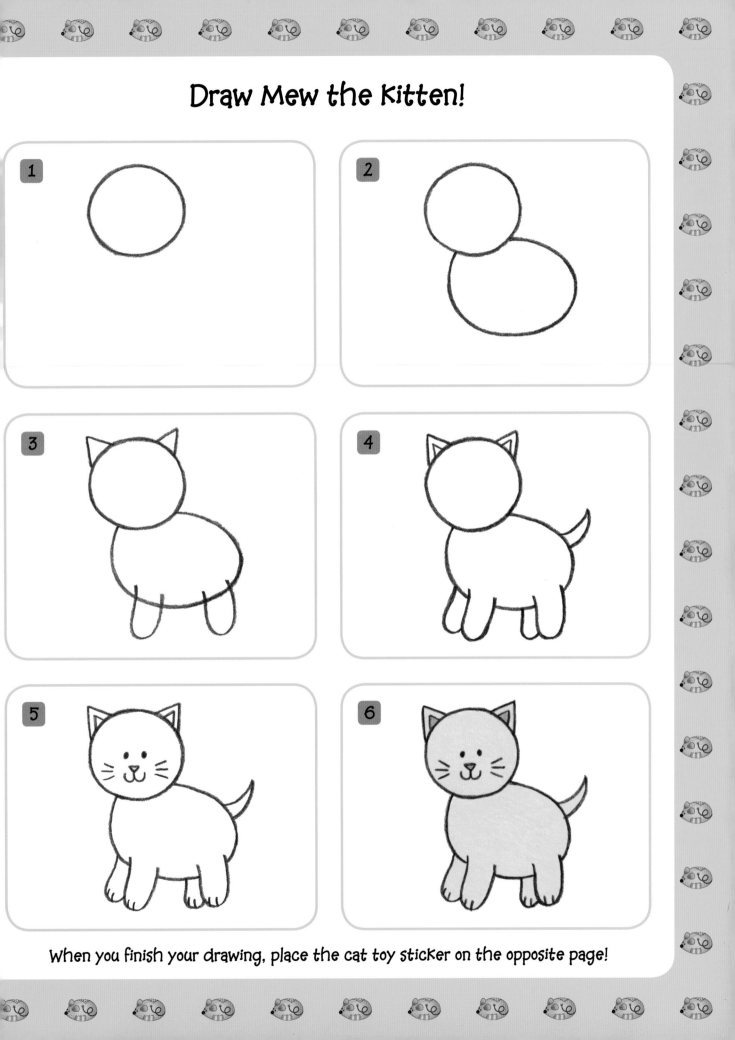

When you finish your drawing, place the cat toy sticker on the opposite page!

Mew is very fond of Gilbert, another member of the Bailey family. But Mew doesn't want to make friends with Gil—she would like nothing better than to eat the little fish! So Boomer carefully watches over Gil to make sure he is safe, which means that Boomer is there to take the blame when Mr. Bailey discovers the water Mew spilled. "BOO-MER!"

Draw Gilbert the fish!

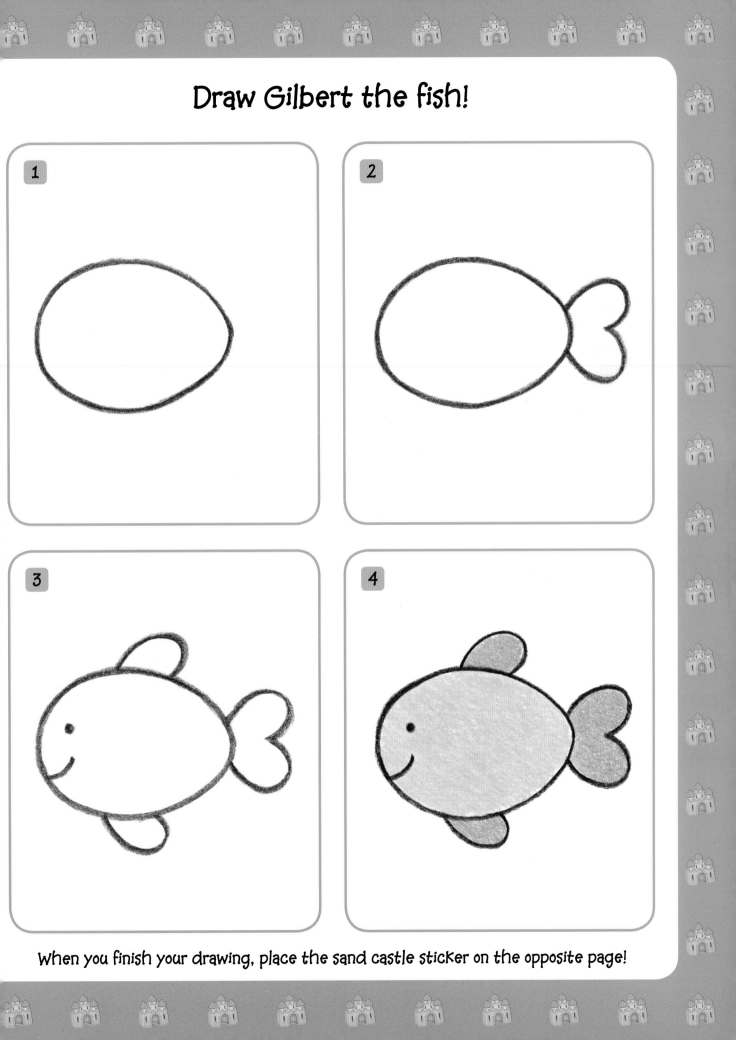

When you finish your drawing, place the sand castle sticker on the opposite page!

While Boomer is being scolded for the fish bowl disaster, Mew scampers upstairs, where she finds even more trouble. Mew tries to squeeze her paw through the bars of Squawk's cage! When Boomer hears the parakeet call for help, he runs in to chase Mew away. So only Boomer is there to blame when Mrs. Bailey comes to the ruffled bird's rescue. "BOO-MER!"

Draw Squawk the parakeet!

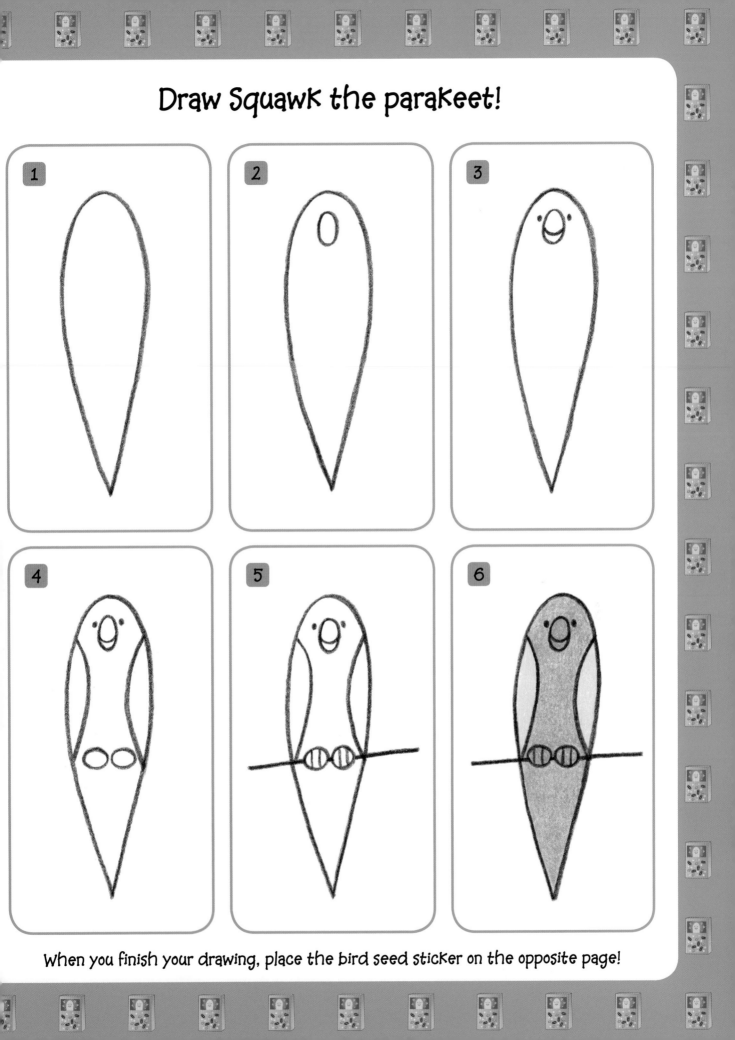

When you finish your drawing, place the bird seed sticker on the opposite page!

To keep Boomer out of trouble, the Baileys send him to the backyard. But what does he find just outside the door? Mew, again—and this time she is climbing the bunny hutch! In an effort to save his friend Whiskers, Boomer makes a dash for Mew. But she bounds off, and the bunny hutch comes tumbling down. When the Baileys find Boomer with Whiskers, you can imagine what they think! "BOO-MER!"

Draw Whiskers the bunny!

When you finish your drawing, place the carrot sticker on the opposite page!

Boomer seems to be causing so much trouble that the Baileys decide to put him in the laundry room for a "time out." Boomer sighs. At least Iggy the iguana is there to Keep him company. Or Iggy would have been there, if he hadn't slithered out the door when Boomer entered. Once Mr. Bailey finds Iggy in the bathtub, he blames Boomer. "BOO-MER!"

Draw Iggy the iguana!

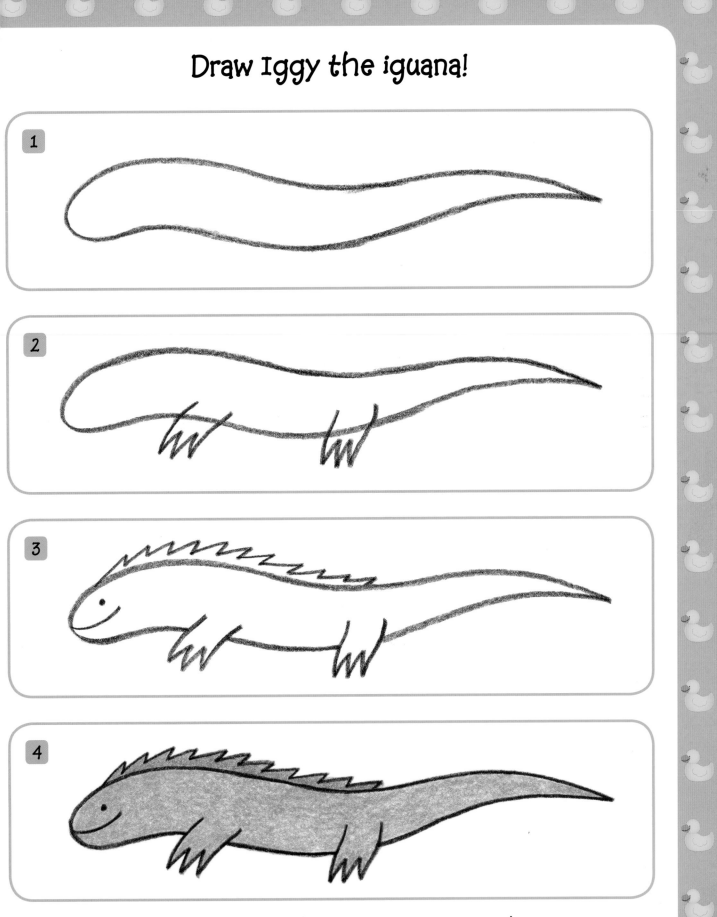

1

2

3

4

When you finish your drawing, place the rubber ducky sticker on the opposite page!

Mr. Bailey sends Boomer back outside. There, Boomer spots Houdini the tortoise. Houdini is finally coming out of hibernation, but he is struggling to climb out of the hole where he slept all winter. Boomer offers to help. But Mrs. Bailey doesn't quite understand the circumstances when she sees Boomer digging in the garden. "BOO-MER!"

Draw Houdini the tortoise!

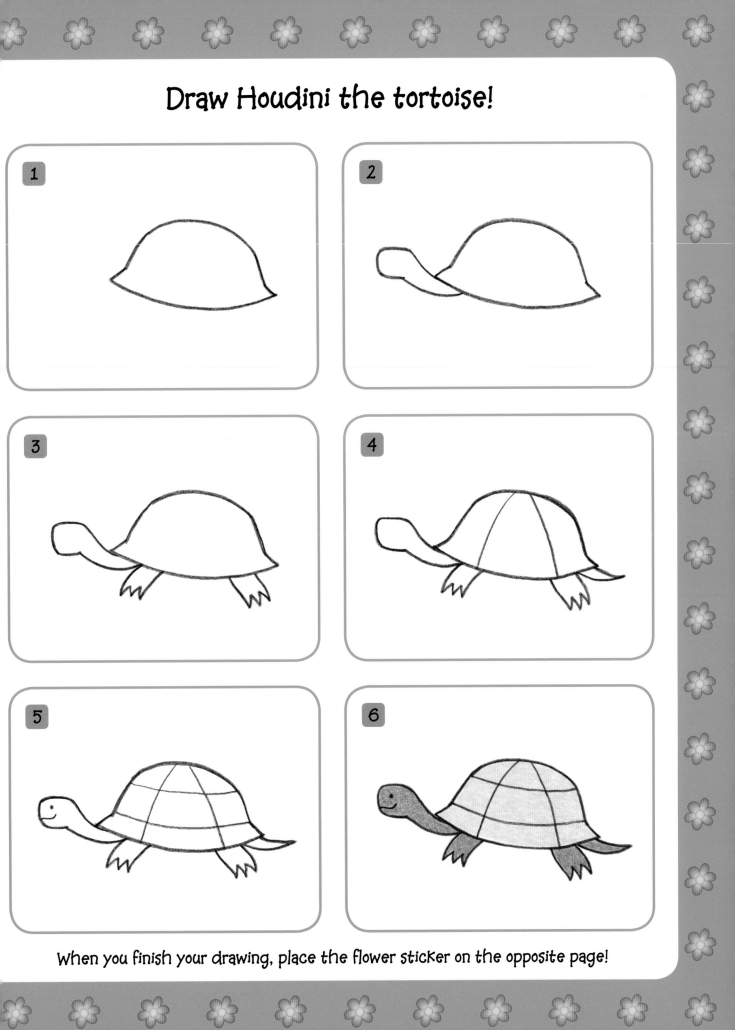

When you finish your drawing, place the flower sticker on the opposite page!

"I'm sorry, Boomer," says Mrs. Bailey, "but I'm going to have to tie you up to keep you out of trouble." Mrs. Bailey ties Boomer's leash to a tree in the corner of the yard. So when Boomer spots Mew chasing Crackers, the family duck, all he can do is bark in alarm. "BOO-MER!" yells Mrs. Bailey, "Stop making so much noise!" Of course, she blames Boomer.

Draw Crackers the duck!

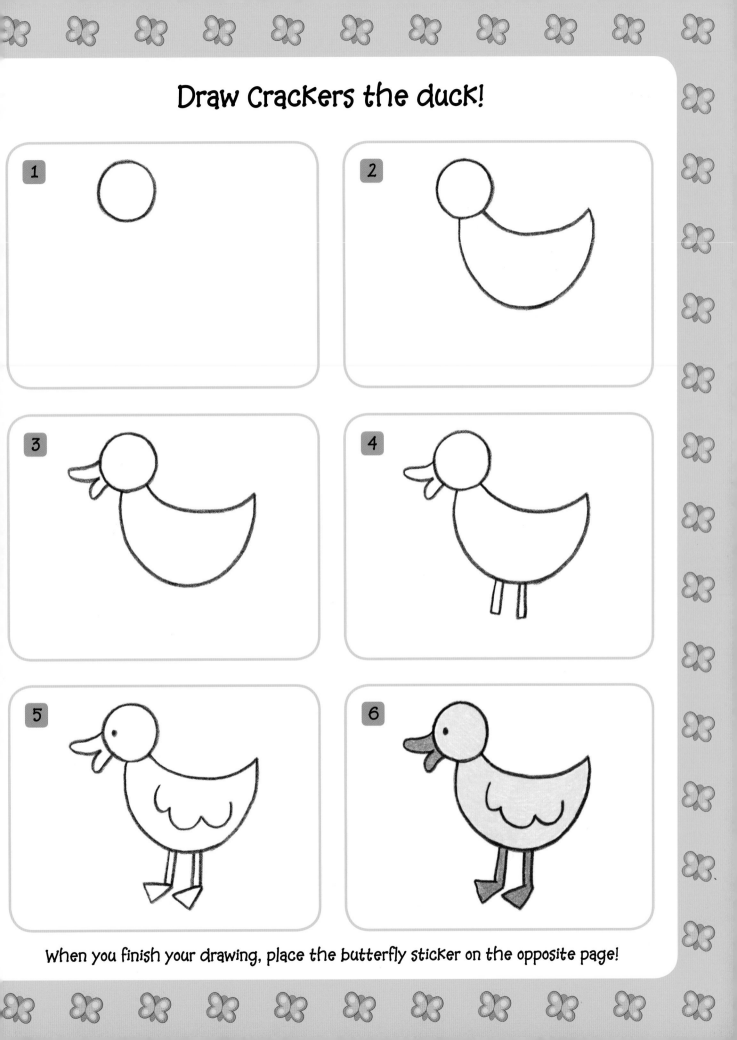

When you finish your drawing, place the butterfly sticker on the opposite page!

Boomer is frustrated that he can't keep an eye on things, especially while Mew is on the loose! Thankfully, Mr. Bailey comes out to the yard. But Mr. Bailey doesn't unleash Boomer. Instead, he ties up Hamlet, the pot-bellied pig. Mr. Bailey grumbles about muddy smudges on the carpet, forgetting that it was Mew that chased Crackers through the mud. Poor Hamlet!

Draw Hamlet the pot-bellied pig!

When you finish your drawing, place the water bowl sticker on the opposite page!

Boomer is surprised that the blame for the mud hasn't fallen on him! He is even more surprised when Bandit, the family ferret, comes scurrying out of the house with Mrs. Bailey hot on his heels. Bandit darts past the tree, but Mrs. Bailey stops there. "Boomer!" gasps Mrs. Bailey, "I could really use your help catching Bandit!"

Draw Bandit the ferret!

When you finish your drawing, place the dog bone sticker on the opposite page!

When Mrs. Bailey releases Boomer, he races inside to the hamster cage, where Dizzy is running on her wheel. Sure enough, Bandit dives for cover behind the cage—but Boomer quickly catches the ferret by the scruff of the neck, without interrupting Dizzy's daily exercise. Boomer receives a big hug and a pat from Mrs. Bailey. "Boomer," she says, "what would we ever do without you?"

Draw Dizzy the hamster!

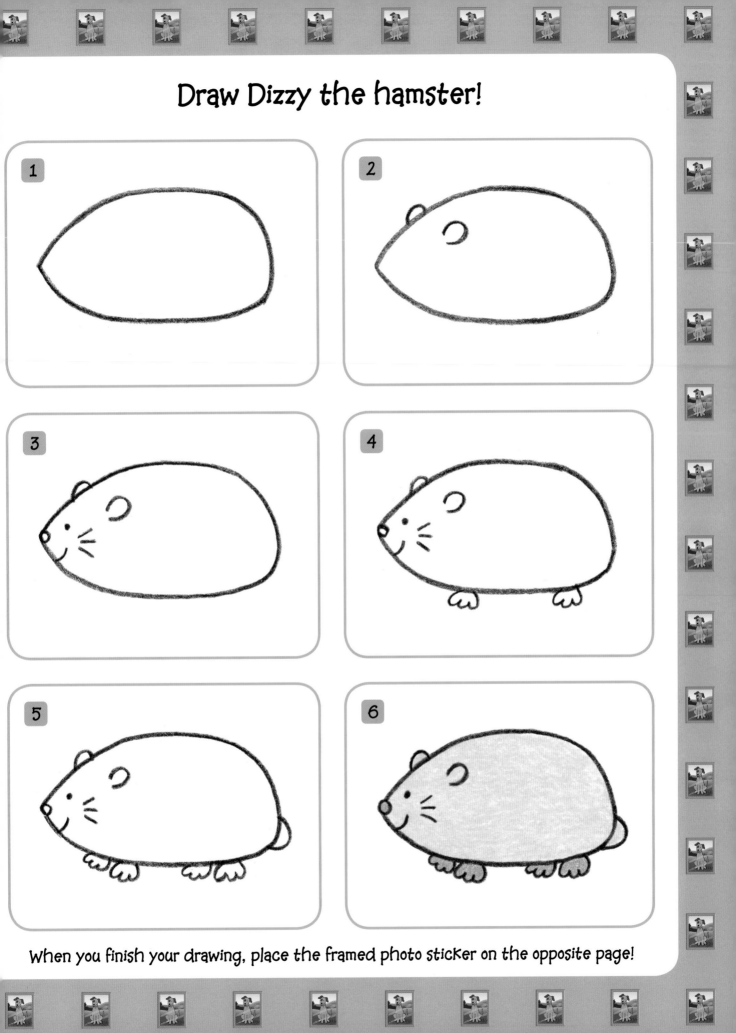

When you finish your drawing, place the framed photo sticker on the opposite page!

The end.

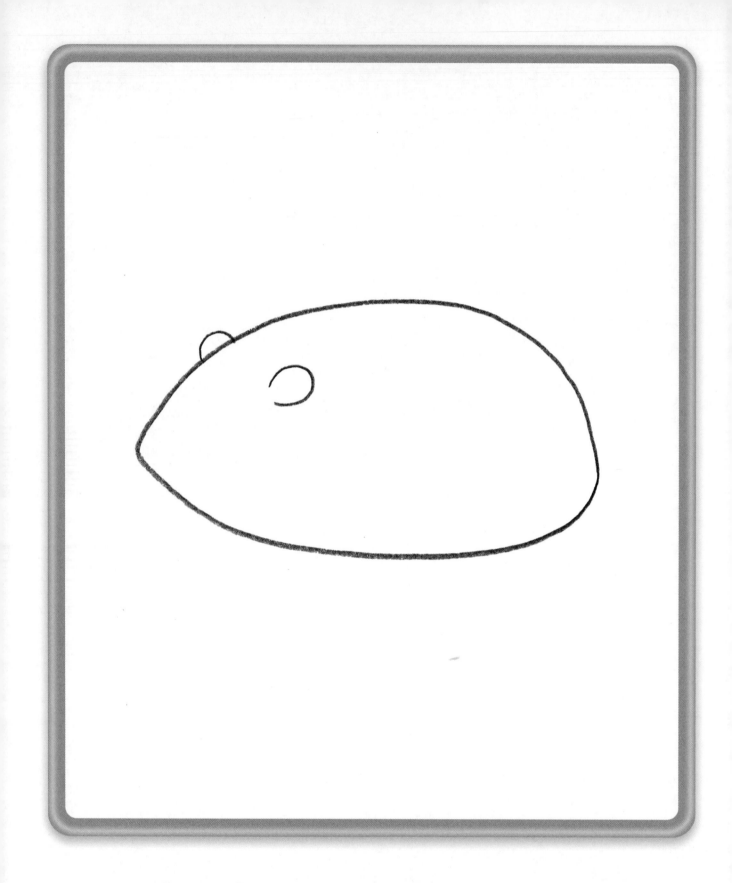

Add Dizzy's face. Then draw her four feet, making three toes on each foot. Finish with her tail.

Give Bandit front and back paws. Draw his tail. Then add the lines between his toes.

Add Hamlet's tail. Draw his nostrils, eyes,
and smile. Then finish his hooves.

Draw Crackers' legs. Then
add his feet, wing, and eye.

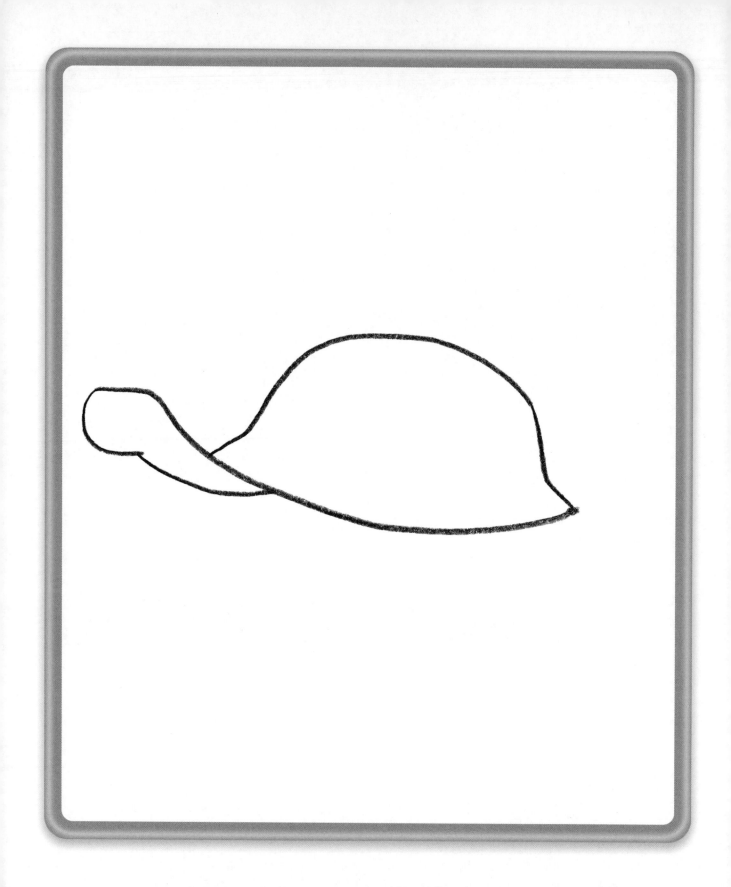

Draw Houdini's legs. Add the first stripes to his shell. Draw his tail. Then finish his face and shell.

Make zigzags for Iggy's scales.
Then draw his face.

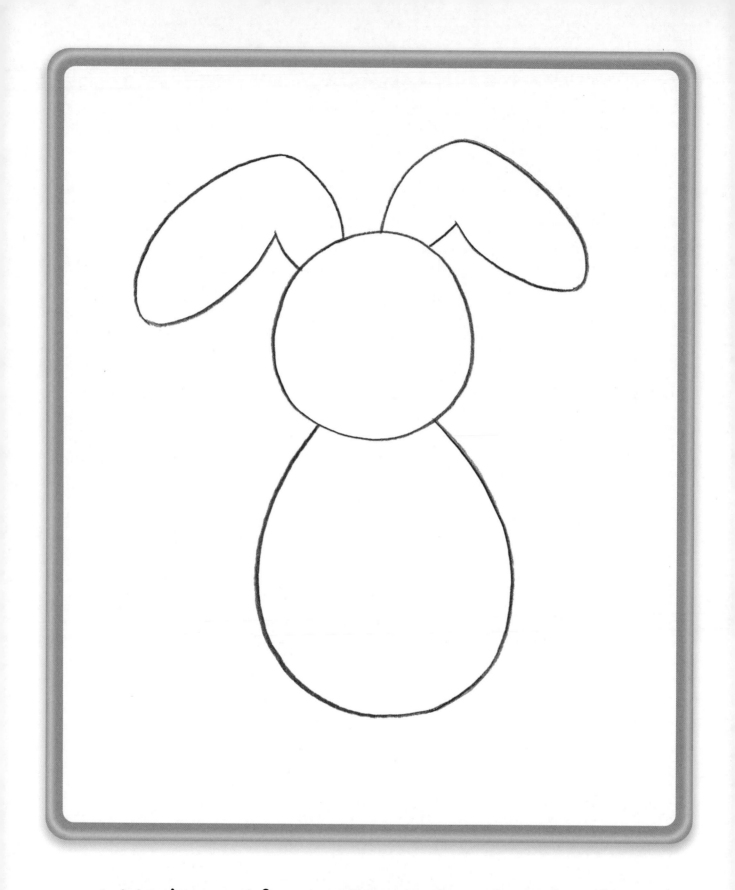

Add Whiskers' front and back paws. Draw her face
and whiskers. And add lines between her toes.

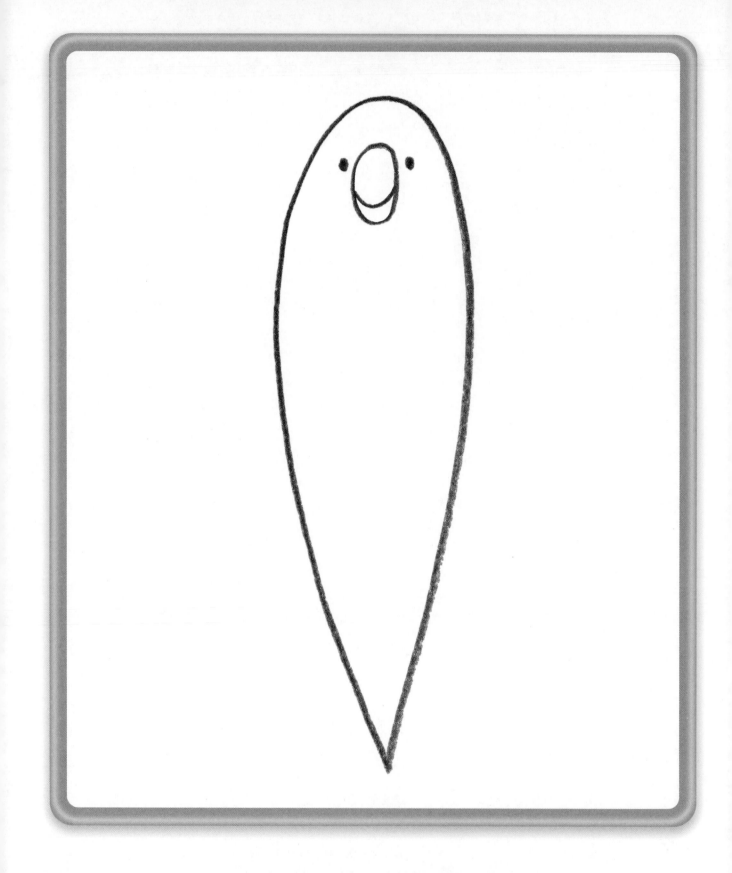

Draw Squawk's wings and feet.
Next add her perch.

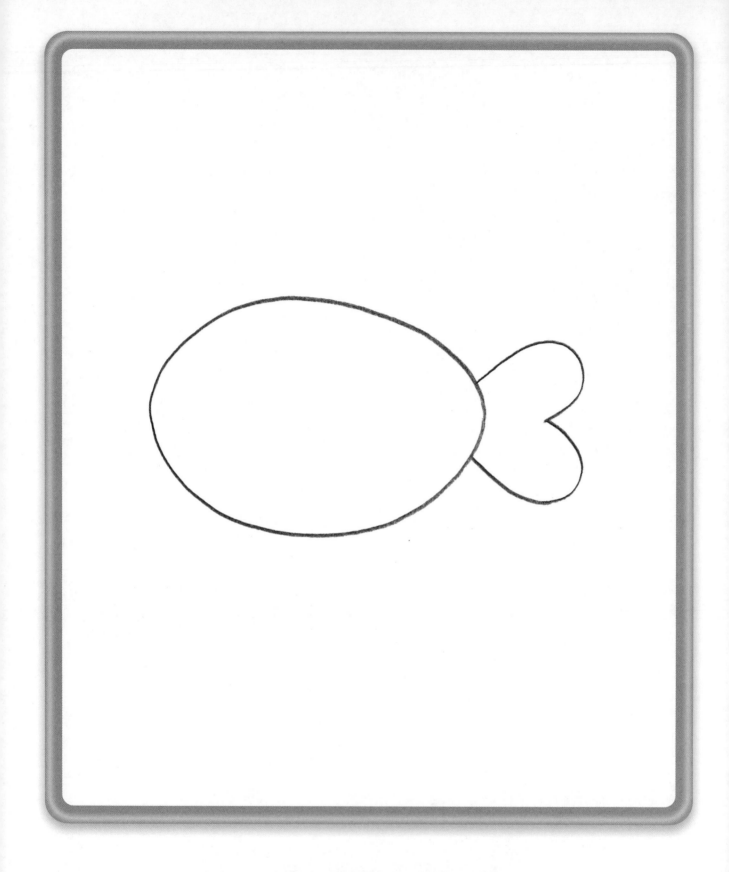

Draw Gilbert's top and bottom
fins. Next add his face.

Add Mew's eyes, nose, mouth, and whiskers.
Then draw lines between her toes.

Draw Boomer's tail and legs.
Then add his eyes and nose.